Catharine

Jane Austen

A Phoenix Paperback

This lightly modernised edition published in 1996 by Phoenix
a division of Orion Books Ltd
Orion House, 5 Upper St Martin's Lane, London WC2H 9EA

Typeset by Deltatype Ltd, Ellesmere Port, Cheshire
Printed in Great Britain by Clays Ltd, St Ives plc

ISBN 1 85799 751 4

Catharine
(or the Bower)

To Miss Austen

Madam

Encouraged by your warm patronage of The beautiful Cassandra, and The History of England, which through your generous support, have obtained a place in every library in the Kingdom, and run through threescore Editions, I take the liberty of begging the same Exertions in favour of the following Novel, which I humbly flatter myself, possesses Merit beyond any already published, or any that will ever in future appear, except such as may proceed from the pen of Your Most Grateful Humble Serv[t]

The Author

Steventon August 1792

Catharine had the misfortune, as many heroines have had before her, of losing her parents when she was very young, and of being brought up under the care of a maiden aunt, who while she tenderly loved her, watched over her conduct with so scrutinizing a severity, as to make it very doubtful to many people, and to Catharine amongst the rest, whether she loved her or not. She had frequently been deprived of a real pleasure through this jealous caution, had been sometimes obliged to relinquish a ball because an officer was to be there, or to dance with a partner of her aunt's introduction in preference to one of her own choice. But her spirits were naturally good, and not easily depressed, and she possessed such a fund of vivacity and good humour as could only be damped by some very serious vexation. – Besides these antidotes against every disappointment, and consolations under them, she had another, which afforded her constant relief in all her misfortunes, and that was a fine shady bower, the work of her own infantine labours assisted by those of two young companions who had resided in the same village – . To this bower, which terminated a very pleasant and retired walk in her aunt's garden, she always wandered whenever anything disturbed her, and it possessed such a charm over her senses, as constantly to tranquillize her mind and quiet her spirits – Solitude and reflection might perhaps have had the same effect in her bed chamber, yet habit had so strengthened the idea which fancy had first suggested, that such a thought never occurred to Kitty who was firmly persuaded that her bower alone could restore her to herself. Her imagination was warm, and in her friendships, as well as in the whole tenure of her mind, she was enthusiastic. This beloved bower had been the united work of herself and two amiable girls, for whom since her earliest years, she had felt the tenderest regard. They were the daughters of the clergyman of the parish with whose family, while it had continued there, her aunt had been on the most intimate terms, and the little girls tho' separated for the greatest part of the year by the different modes of their education, were constantly together during the holidays of the Miss Wynnes. In those days of happy childhood, now so often regretted by Kitty, this arbour had been formed, and separated perhaps for ever from these dear friends, it encouraged more than any other place the tender and melancholy recollections of hours rendered pleasant by *them*, at once so sorrowful, yet so soothing! It was now two years since the death of Mr Wynne, and the consequent dispersion of his family who had been left by it in great distress. They had been reduced to a state of absolute dependance on some relations, who though very opulent and very nearly connected with them, had with difficulty been prevailed on to contribute anything towards their support. Mrs Wynne was fortunately spared the knowledge and participation of their distress, by her release from a painful illness a few months before the death of her husband. – The eldest daughter had been obliged to accept the offer of one of her cousins to equip her for the East Indies, and tho' infinitely against her inclinations had been necessitated to embrace the only possibility that was offered to her, of a maintenance. Yet it was *one*, so opposite to all her ideas of propriety, so contrary to her wishes, so repugnant to her feelings, that she would almost have preferred servitude to it, had choice been allowed her – .

Her personal attractions had gained her a husband as soon as she had arrived at Bengal, and she had now been married nearly a twelve month. Splendidly, yet unhappily married. United to a man of double her own age, whose disposition was not amiable, and whose manners were unpleasing, though his character was respectable. Kitty had heard twice from her friend since her marriage, but her letters were always unsatisfactory, and though she did not openly avow her feelings, yet every line proved her to be unhappy. She spoke with pleasure of nothing, but of those amusements which they had shared together and which could return no more, and seemed to have no happiness in view but that of returning to England again. Her sister had been taken by another relation the Dowager Lady Halifax as a companion to her daughters, and had accompanied her family into Scotland about the same time of Cecilia's leaving England. From Mary therefore Kitty had the power of hearing more frequently, but her letters were scarcely more comfortable – . There was not indeed that hopelessness of sorrow in her situation as in her sister's; she was not married, and could yet look forward to a change in her circumstances, but situated for the present without any immediate hope of it, in a family where, tho' all were her relations she had no friend, she wrote usually in depressed spirits, which her separation from her sister and her sister's marriage had greatly contributed to make so. – Divided thus from the two she loved best on Earth, while Cecilia and Mary were still more endeared to her by their loss, everything that brought a remembrance of them was doubly cherished, and the shrubs they had planted, and the keepsakes they had given were rendered sacred – . The living of Chetwynde was now in the possession of a Mr Dudley, whose family unlike the Wynnes were productive only of vexation and trouble to Mrs Percival and her niece. Mr Dudley, who was the younger son of a very noble family, of a family more famed for their pride than their opulence, tenacious of his dignity, and jealous of his rights, was forever quarrelling, if not with Mrs Percival herself, with her steward and tenants concerning tithes, and with the principal neighbours themselves concerning the respect and parade, he exacted. His wife, an ill-educated, untaught woman of ancient family, was proud of that family almost without knowing why, and like him too was haughty and quarrelsome, without considering for what. Their only daughter, who inherited the ignorance, the insolence, and pride of her parents, was from that beauty of which she was unreasonably vain, considered by them as an irresistible creature, and looked up to as the future restorer, by a Splendid Marriage, of the dignity which their reduced situation and Mr Dudley's being obliged to take orders for a country living had so much lessened. They at once despised the Percivals as people of mean family, and envied them as people of fortune. They were jealous of their being more respected than themselves and while they affected to consider them as of no consequence, were continually seeking to lessen them in the opinion of the neighbourhood by scandalous and malicious reports. Such a family as this, was ill-calculated to console Kitty for the loss of the Wynnes, or to fill up by their society, those occasionally irksome hours which in so retired a situation would sometimes occur for want of a companion. Her aunt was most excessively fond of her, and miserable if she saw her for a moment out of spirits; Yet she lived in such constant apprehension of her marrying imprudently if she were allowed the opportunity of choosing, and was so dissatisfied with her behaviour when she saw her with young men, for it was, from her natural disposition remarkably open and unreserved, that though she frequently wished for her niece's sake, that the neighbourhood were larger, and that she had used herself to mix more with it, yet the recollection of there being young men in almost every family in it, always conquered the wish. The same fears that prevented Mrs Percival's joining much in the society of her neighbours, led her equally to avoid inviting her relations to spend any time in her house – she had therefore constantly regretted the annual attempt of a distant relation to visit her at Chetwynde, as there was a young man in the family of whom she had heard many traits that alarmed her. This son was however now on his travels, and the repeated solicitations of Kitty, joined to a consciousness of having declined with too little ceremony the frequent overtures of her friends to be admitted, and a real wish to see them herself, easily prevailed on her to press with great earnestness the pleasure of a visit from them during the summer. Mr and Mrs Stanley were accordingly to come, and Catharine, in having an object to look forward to, a something to expect that must inevitably relieve the dullness of a constant tête à tête with her aunt, was so delighted, and her spirits so elevated, that for the three or four days immediately preceding their arrival, she could scarcely fix herself to any employment. In this point Mrs Percival always thought her defective, and frequently complained of a want of steadiness and perseverance in her occupations, which were by no means congenial to the eagerness of Kitty's disposition, and perhaps not often met with in any young person. The tediousness too of her aunt's conversation and the want of agreeable companions greatly increased this desire of change in her employments, for Kitty found herself much sooner tired of reading, working, or drawing, in Mrs Percival's parlour than in her own arbour, where Mrs Percival for fear of its being damp never accompanied her.

As her aunt prided herself on the exact propriety and neatness with which everything in her family was conducted, and had no highter satisfaction than that of knowing her house to be always in complete order, as her fortune was good, and her establishment ample, few were the preparations necessary for the reception of her visitors. The day of their arrival so long expected, at length came, and the noise of the coach and as it drove round the sweep, was to Catharine a more interesting sound, than the music of an Italian opera, which to most heroines is the height of enjoyment. Mr and Mrs Stanley were people of large fortune and high fashion. He was a Member of the House of Commons, and they were therefore most agreeably necessitated to reside half the year in Town; where Miss Stanley had been attended by the most capital masters from the time of her being six years old to the last spring, which comprehending a period of twelve years had been dedicated to the acquirement of accomplishments which were now to be displayed and in a few years entirely neglected. She was elegant in her appearance, rather handsome, and naturally not deficient in abilities; but those years which ought to have been spent in the attainment of useful knowledge and mental improvement, had been all bestowed in learning drawing, Italian and music, more especially the latter, and she now united to these accomplishments, an understanding unimproved by reading and a mind totally devoid either of taste or judgement. Her temper was by nature good, but unassisted by reflection, she had neither patience under disappointment, nor could sacrifice her own inclinations to promote the happiness of others. All her ideas were towards the elegance of her appearance, the fashion of her dress, and the admiration she wished them to excite. She professed a love of books without reading, was lively without wit, and generally good humoured without merit. Such was Camilla Stanley; and Catharine, who was prejudiced by her appearance, and who from her solitary situation was ready to like anyone, tho' her understanding and judgement would not otherwise have been easily satisfied, felt almost convinced when she saw her, that Miss

Stanley would be the very companion she wanted, and in some degree make amends for the loss of Cecilia and Mary Wynne. She therefore attached herself to Camilla from the first day of her arrival, and from being the only young people in the house, they were by inclination constant companions. Kitty was herself a great reader, tho' perhaps not a very deep one, and felt therefore highly delighted to find that Miss Stanley was equally fond of it. Eager to know that their sentiments as to books were similar, she very soon began questioning her new acquaintance on the subject; but though she was well read in modern history herself, she chose rather to speak first of books of a lighter kind, of books universally read and admired.

'You have read Mrs Smith's novels, I suppose?' said she to her companion – . 'Oh! Yes,' replied the other, 'and I am quite delighted with them – They are the sweetest things in the world – ' 'And which do you prefer of them?' 'Oh! dear, I think there is no comparison between them – *Emmeline* is *so much* better than any of the others – ' 'Many people think so, I know; but there does not appear so great a disproportion in their merits to *me*; do you think it is better written?' 'Oh! I do not know anything about *that* – but it is better in *every thing* – Besides, *Ethelinde* is so long – ' 'That is a very common objection I believe,' said Kitty, 'but for my own part, if a book is well written, I always find it too short.' 'So do I, only I get tired of it before it is finished.' 'But did not you find the story of *Ethelinde* very interesting? And the descriptions of Grasmere, are not they beautiful?' 'Oh! I missed them all, because I was in such a hurry to know the end of it' – . Then from an easy transition she added, 'We are going to the Lakes this autumn, and I am quite mad with joy; Sir Henry Devereux has promised to go with us, and that will make it so pleasant, you know – '

'I dare say it will; but I think it is a pity that Sir Henry's powers of pleasing were not reserved for an occasion where they might be more wanted. – However I quite envy you the pleasure of such a scheme.'

'Oh! I am quite delighted with the thoughts of it; I can think of nothing else. I assure you I have done nothing for this last month but plan what clothes I should take with me, and I have at last determined to take very few indeed besides my travelling dress, and so I advise you to do, when ever you go; for I intend in case we should fall in with any races, or stop at Matlock or Scarborough, to have some things made for the occasion.'

'You intend then to go into Yorkshire?'

'I believe not – indeed I know nothing of the route, for I never trouble myself about such things. I only know that we are to go from Derbyshire to Matlock and Scarborough, but to which of them first, I neither know nor care – I am in hopes of meeting some particular friends of mine at Scarborough – Augusta told me in her last letter that Sir Peter talked of going; but then you know that is so uncertain. I cannot bear Sir Peter, he is such a horrid creature – '

 'He *is*, is he?' said Kitty, not knowing what else to say.

'Oh! he is quite shocking.' Here the conversation was interrupted, and Kitty was left in a painful uncertainty, as to the particulars of Sir Peter's character; she knew only that he was horrid and shocking, but why, and in what, yet remained to be discovered. She could scarcely resolve what to think of her new acquaintance; she appeared to be shamefully ignorant as to the geography of England, if she had understood her right, and equally devoid of taste and information. Kitty was however unwilling to decide hastily; she was at once desirous of doing Miss Stanley justice, and of having her own wishes in her answered; she determined therefore to suspend all judgement for some time. After supper, the conversation turning on the state of affairs in the political world, Mrs Percival, who was firmly of opinion that the whole race of mankind were degenerating, said that for her part, everything she believed was going to rack and ruin, all order was destroyed over the face of the World, the House of Commons she heard did not break up sometimes till five in the morning, and depravity never was so general before; concluding with a wish that she might live to see the manners of the people in Queen Elizabeth's reign, restored again. 'Well, ma'am,' said her niece, 'but I hope you do not mean with the times to restore Queen Elizabeth herself.'

'Queen Elizabeth,' said Mrs Stanley, who never hazarded a remark on history that was not well founded, 'lived to a good old age, and was a very clever woman.' 'True, ma'am,' said Kitty; 'but I do not consider either of those circumstances as meritorious in herself, and they are very far from making me wish her return, for if she were to come again with the same abilities and the same good constitution she might do as much mischief and last as long as she did before – .' Then turning to Camilla who had been sitting very silent for some time, she added, 'What do *you* think of Elizabeth, Miss Stanley? I hope you will not defend her.'

'Oh! dear,' said Miss Stanley, 'I know nothing of politics, and cannot bear to hear them mentioned.' Kitty started at this repulse, but made no answer; that Miss Stanley must be ignorant of what she could not distinguish from politics she felt perfectly convinced. – She retired to her own room, perplexed in her opinion about her new acquaintance, and fearful of her being very unlike Cecilia and Mary. She arose the next morning to experience a fuller conviction of this, and every future day increased it – . She found no variety in her conversation; She received no information from her but in fashions, and no amusement but in her performance on the harpsichord; and after repeated endeavours to find her what she wished, she was obliged to give up the attempt and to consider it as fruitless. There had occasionally appeared a something like humour in Camilla which had inspired her with hopes, that she might at least have a natural genius, tho' not an improved one, but these sparklings of wit happened so seldom, and were so ill-supported that she was at last convinced of their being merely accidental. All her stock of knowledge was exhausted in a very few days, and when Kitty had learnt from her, how large their house in

 Town was, when the fashionable amusements began, who

were the celebrated beauties and who the best milliner, Camilla had nothing further to teach, except the characters of any of her acquaintance as they occurred in conversation, which was done with equal ease and brevity, by saying that the person was either the sweetest creature in the world, and one of whom she was dotingly fond, or horrid, shocking and not fit to be seen.

As Catharine was very desirous of gaining every possible information as to the characters of the Halifax family, and concluded that Miss Stanley must be acquainted with them, as she seemed to be so with every one of any consequence, she took an opportunity as Camilla was one day enumerating all the people of rank that her mother visited, of asking her whether Lady Halifax were among the number.

'Oh! Thank you for reminding me of her; she is the sweetest woman in the world, and one of our most intimate acquaintance, I do not suppose there is a day passes during the six months that we are in Town, but what we see each other in the course of it – . And I correspond with all the girls.'

'They *are* then a very pleasant family?' said Kitty. 'They ought to be so indeed, to allow of such frequent meetings, or all conversation must be at end.'

'Oh! dear, not at all,' said Miss Stanley, 'for sometimes we do not speak to each other for a month together. We meet perhaps only in public, and then you know we are often not able to get near enough; but in that case we always nod and smile.'

'Which does just as well – . But I was going to ask you whether you have ever seen a Miss Wynne with them?'

'I know who you mean perfectly – she wears a blue hat – . I have frequently seen her in Brook Street, when I have been at Lady Halifax's balls – she gives one every month during the winter – . But only think how good it is in her to take care of Miss Wynne, for she is a very distant relation, and so poor that, as Miss Halifax told me, her Mother was obliged to find her in clothes. Is not it shameful?'

'That she should be so poor? it is indeed, with such wealthy connexions as the family have.'

'Oh! no; I mean, was not it shameful in Mr Wynne to leave his children so distressed, when he had actually the living of Chetwynde and two or three curacies, and only four children to provide for – . What would he have done if he had had ten, as many people have?'

'He would have given them all a good education and have left them all equally poor.'

'Well I do think there never was so lucky a family. Sir George Fitzgibbon you know sent the eldest girl to India entirely at his own expense, where they say she is most nobly married and the happiest creature in the world – Lady Halifax you see has taken care of the youngest and treats her as if she were her daughter; She does not go out into public with her to be sure; but then she is always present when her Ladyship gives her balls, and nothing can be kinder to her than Lady Halifax is; she would have taken her to Cheltenham last year, if there had been room enough at the lodgings, and therefore I do not think that *she* can have anything to complain of. Then there are the two sons; one of them the Bishop of M—— has got into the Army as a Lieutenant I suppose; and the other is extremely well off I know, for I have a notion that somebody puts him to school somewhere in Wales. Perhaps you knew them when they lived here?'

'Very well, we met as often as your family and the Halifaxes do in Town, but as we seldom had any difficulty in getting near enough to speak, we seldom parted with merely a nod and a smile. They were indeed a most charming family, and I believe have scarcely their equals in the world; the neighbours we now have at the Parsonage, appear to more disadvantage in coming after them.'

'Oh! horrid wretches! I wonder you can endure them.'

'Why, what would you have one do?'

'Oh! Lord, If I were in your place, I should abuse them all day long.'

'So I do, but it does no good.'

'Well, I declare it is quite a pity that they should be suffered to live. I wish my father would propose knocking all their brains out, some day or other when he is in the House. So abominably proud of their family! And I dare say after all, that there is nothing particular in it.'

'Why yes, I believe they *have* reason to value themselves on it, if any body has; for you know he is Lord Amyatt's brother.'

'Oh! I know all that very well, but it is no reason for their being so horrid. I remember I met Miss Dudley last spring with Lady Amyatt at Ranelagh, and she had such a frightful cap on, that I have never been able to bear any of them since. – And so you used to think the Wynnes very pleasant?'

'You speak as if their being so were doubtful! Pleasant! Oh! they were every thing that could interest and attach. It is not in my power to do justice to their merits, tho' not to feel them, I think must be impossible. They have unfitted me for any society but their own!'

'Well, that is just what I think of the Miss Halifaxes; by the bye, I must write to Caroline tomorrow, and I do not know what to say to her. The Barlows too are just such other sweet girls; but I wish Augusta's hair was not so dark. I cannot bear Sir Peter – horrid wretch! He is *always* laid up with the gout, which is exceedingly disagreeable to the family.'

'And perhaps not very pleasant to *himself* – . But as to the Wynnes; do you really think them very fortunate?'

'Do I? Why, does not every body? Miss Halifax and Caroline and Maria all say that they are the luckiest creatures in the world. So does Sir George Fitzgibbon and so do every body.'

'That is, every body who have themselves conferred an obligation on them. But do you call it lucky, for a girl of genius and feeling to be sent in quest of a husband to Bengal, to be married there to a man of whose disposition she has no opportunity of judging till her judgement is of no use to her, who may be a tyrant, or a fool or both for what she knows to the contrary. Do you call *that* fortunate?'

'I know nothing of all that; I only know that it was extremely good in Sir George to fit her out and pay her passage, and that she would not have found many who would have done the same.'

'I wish she had not found *one*,' said Kitty with great eagerness, 'she might then have remained in England and been happy.'

'Well, I cannot conceive the hardship of going out in a very agreeable manner with two or three sweet girls for companions, having a delightful voyage to Bengal or Barbadoes or wherever it is, and being married soon after one's arrival to a very charming man immensely rich –. I see no hardship in all that.'

'Your representation of the affair,' said Kitty laughing, 'certainly gives a very different idea of it from mine. But supposing all this to be true, still, as it was by no means certain that she would be so fortunate either in her voyage, her companions, or her husband; in being obliged to run the risk of their proving very different, she undoubtedly experienced a great hardship – . Besides, to a girl of any delicacy, the voyage in itself, since the object of it is so universally known, is a punishment that needs no other to make it very severe.'

'I do not see that at all. She is not the first girl who has gone to the East Indies for a husband, and I declare I should think it very good fun if I were as poor.'

'I believe you would think very differently *then*. But at

least you will not defend her sister's situation? Dependant even for her clothes on the bounty of others, who of course do not pity her, as by your own account, they consider her as very fortunate.'

'You are extremely nice upon my word; Lady Halifax is a delightful woman, and one of the sweetest tempered creatures in the world; I am sure I have every reason to speak well of her, for we are under most amazing obligations to her. She has frequently chaperoned me when my mother has been indisposed, and last spring she lent me her own horse three times, which was a prodigious favour, for it is the most beautiful creature that ever was seen, and I am the only person she ever lent it to.'

'And then,' continued she, 'the Miss Halifaxes are quite delightful. Maria is one of the cleverest girls that ever were known – draws in oils, and plays anything by sight. She promised me one of her drawings before I left Town, but I entirely forgot to ask her for it. I would give anything to have one.'

'But was not it very odd,' said Kitty, 'that the Bishop should send Charles Wynne to sea, when he must have had a much better chance of providing for him in the Church, which was the profession that Charles liked best, and the one for which his father had intended him? The Bishop I know had often promised Mr Wynne a living, and as he never gave him one, I think it was incumbent on him to transfer the promise to his son.'

 'I believe you think he ought to have resigned his

Bishopric to him; you seem determined to be dissatisfied with every thing that has been done for them.'

'Well,' said Kitty, 'this is a subject on which we shall never agree, and therefore it will be useless to continue it farther, or to mention it again – ' She then left the room, and running out of the house was soon in her dear bower where she could indulge in peace all her affectionate anger against the relations of the Wynnes, which was greatly heightened by finding from Camilla that they were in general considered as having acted particularly well by them – . She amused herself for some time in abusing, and hating them all, with great spirit, and when this tribute to her regard for the Wynnes, was paid, and the bower began to have its usual influence over her spirits, she contributed towards settling them, by taking out a book, for she had always one about her, and reading – . She had been so employed for nearly an hour, when Camilla came running towards her with great eagerness, and apparently great pleasure – . 'Oh! my dear Catharine,' said she, half out of breath – 'I have such delightful news for you – But you shall guess what it is – We are all the happiest creatures in the world; would you believe it, the Dudleys have sent us an invitation to a ball at their own house – . What charming people they are! I had no idea of there being so much sense in the whole family – I declare I quite dote upon them – . And it happens so fortunately too, for I expect a new cap from Town tomorrow which will just do for a ball – gold net – It will be a most angelic thing – every body will be longing for the pattern – '. The expectation of a ball was indeed very agreeable intelligence to Kitty, who fond of dancing and seldom able to enjoy it, had reason to feel even greater pleasure in it than her friend; for to *her*, it was now no novelty – . Camilla's delight however was by no means inferior to Kitty's, and she rather expressed the most of the two. The cap came and every other preparation was soon completed; while these were in agitation the days passed gaily away, but when directions were no longer necessary, taste could no longer be displayed, the difficulties no longer overcome, the short period that intervened before the day of the ball hung heavily on their hands, and every hour was too long. The very few times that Kitty had ever enjoyed the amusement of dancing was an excuse for *her* impatience, and an apology for the idleness it occasioned to a mind naturally very active; but her friend without such a plea was infinitely worse than herself. She could do nothing but wander from the house to the garden, and from the garden to the avenue, wondering when Thursday would come, which she might easily have ascertained, and counting the hours as they passed which served only to lengthen them – .

They retired to their rooms in high spirits on Wednesday night, but Kitty awoke the next morning with a violent toothache. It was in vain that she endeavoured at first to deceive herself; her feelings were witnesses too acute of its reality; with as little success did she try to sleep it off, for the pain she suffered prevented her closing her eyes – . She then summoned her maid and with the assistance of the housekeeper, every remedy that the receipt book or the head of the latter contained, was tried, but ineffectually; for though for a short time relieved by them, the pain still returned. She was now obliged to give up the endeavour, and to reconcile herself not only to the pain of a toothache, but to the loss of a ball; and though she had with so much eagerness looked forward to the day of its arrival, had received such pleasure in the necessary preparations, and promised herself so much delight in it, yet she was not so totally void of philosophy as many girls of her age might have been in her situation. She considered that there were misfortunes of a much greater magnitude than the loss of a ball, experienced every day by some part of mortality, and that the time might come when she would herself look back with wonder and perhaps with envy on her having known no greater vexation. By such reflections as these, she soon reasoned herself into as much resignation and patience as the pain she suffered, would allow of, which after all was the greatest misfortune of the two, and told the sad story when she entered the breakfast room, with tolerable composure. Mrs Percival more grieved for her toothache than her disappointment, as she feared that it would not be possible to prevent her dancing with a *Man* if she went, was eager to try everything that had already been applied to alleviate the pain, while at the same time she declared it was impossible for her to leave the house. Miss Stanley who joined to her concern for her friend, felt a mixture of dread lest her mother's proposal that they should all remain at home, might be accepted, was very violent in her sorrow on the occasion, and though her apprehensions on the subject were soon quieted by Kitty's protesting that sooner than allow any one to stay with her, she would herself go, she continued to lament it with such unceasing vehemence as at last drove Kitty to her own room. Her fears for herself being now entirely dissipated left her more than ever at leisure to pity and persecute her friend who tho' safe when in her own room, was frequently removing from it to some other in hopes of being more free from pain, and then had no opportunity of escaping her – .

'To be sure, there never was anything so shocking,' said Camilla; 'To come on such a day too! For one would not have minded it you know had it been at *any other* time. But it always is so. I never was at a ball in my life, but what something happened to prevent somebody from going! I wish there were no such things a teeth in the world; they are nothing but plagues to one, and I dare say that people might easily invent something to eat with instead of them; poor thing! what pain you are in! I declare it is quite shocking to look at you. But you won't have it out, will you? For Heaven's sake don't; for there is nothing I dread so much. I declare I have rather undergo the greatest tortures in the world than have a tooth drawn. Well! how patiently you do bear it! how can you be so quiet? Lord, if I were in your place I should make such a fuss, there would be no bearing me. I should torment you to death.'

'So you do, as it is,' thought Kitty.

'For my own part, Catharine' said Mrs Percival 'I have not a doubt but that you caught this toothache by sitting so much in that arbour, for it is always damp. I know it has ruined your constitution entirely; and indeed I do not believe it has been of much service to mine; I sat down in it last May to rest myself, and I have never been quite well since – . I shall order John to pull it all down I assure you.'

'I know you will not do that, ma'am,' said Kitty, 'as you must be convinced how unhappy it would make me.'

'You talk very ridiculously, child; it is all whim and nonsense. Why cannot you fancy this room an arbour?'

'Had this room been built by Cecilia and Mary, I should have valued it equally, ma'am, for it is not merely the name of an arbour, which charms me.'

'Why indeed, Mrs Percival,' said Mrs Stanley, 'I must think that Catharine's affection for her bower is the effect of a sensibility that does her credit. I love to see a friendship between young persons and always consider it as a sure mark of an amiable affectionate disposition. I have from Camilla's infancy taught her to think the same, and have taken great pains to introduce her to young people of her own age who were likely to be worthy of her regard. Nothing forms the taste more than sensible and elegant letters – . Lady Halifax thinks just like me – . Camilla corresponds with her daughters, and I believe I may venture to say that they are none of them *the worse* for it.'

These ideas were too modern to suit Mrs Percival who considered a correspondence between girls as productive of no good, and as the frequent origin of imprudence and error by the effect of pernicious advice and bad example. She could not therefore refrain from saying that for her part, she had lived fifty years in the world without having ever had a correspondent, and did not find herself at all the less respectable for it – . Mrs Stanley could say nothing in answer to this, but her daughter who was less governed by propriety, said in her thoughtless way, 'But who knows what you might have been, ma'am, if you *had* had a correspondent; perhaps it would have made you quite a different creature. I declare I would not be without those I have for all the world. It is the greatest delight of my life, and you cannot think how much their letters have formed my taste as Mama says, for I hear from them generally every week.'

'You received a letter from Augusta Barlow to day, did not you, my love?' said her mother – . 'She writes remarkably well I know.'

'Oh! Yes ma'am, the most delightful letter you ever heard of. She sends me a long account of the new Regency walking dress Lady Susan has given her, and it is so beautiful that I am quite dying with envy for it.'

'Well, I am prodigiously happy to hear such pleasing news of my young friend; I have a high regard for Augusta, and most sincerely partake in the general joy on the occasion. But does she say nothing else? it seemed to be a long letter – Are they to be at Scarborough?'

 'Oh! Lord, she never once mentions it, now I recollect it;

and I entirely forgot to ask her when I wrote last. She says nothing indeed except about the Regency.' 'She *must* write well' thought Kitty, 'to make a long letter upon a bonnet and pelisse.' She then left the room tired of listening to a conversation which tho' it might have diverted her had she been well, served only to fatigue and depress her, while in pain. Happy was it for *her*, when the hour of dressing came, for Camilla satisfied with being surrounded by her mother and half the maids in the house did not want her assistance, and was too agreeably employed to want her society. She remained therefore alone in the parlour, till joined by Mr Stanley and her aunt, who however after a few enquiries, allowed her to continue undisturbed and began their usual conversation on politics. This was a subject on which they could never agree, for Mr Stanley who considered himself as perfectly qualified by his seat in the House, to decide on it without hesitation, resolutely maintained that the Kingdom had not for ages been in so flourishing and prosperous a state, and Mrs Percival with equal warmth, tho' perhaps less argument, as vehemently asserted that the whole nation would speedily be ruined, and everything as she expressed herself be at sixes and sevens. It was not however unamusing to Kitty to listen to the dispute, especially as she began then to be more free from pain, and without taking any share in it herself, she found it very entertaining to observe the eagerness with which they both defended their opinions, and could not help thinking that Mr Stanley would not feel more disappointed if her aunt's expectations were fulfilled, than her Aunt would be mortified by their failure. After waiting a considerable time Mrs Stanley and her daughter appeared, and Camilla in high spirits, and perfect good humour with her own looks, was more violent than ever in her lamentations over her friend as she practised her Scotch steps about the room – . At length they departed, and Kitty better able to amuse herself than she had been the whole day before, wrote a long account of her misfortunes to Mary Wynne.

When her letter was concluded she had an opportunity of witnessing the truth of that assertion which says that sorrows are lightened by communication, for her toothache was then so much relieved that she began to entertain an idea of following her friends to Mr Dudley's. They had been gone an hour, and as every thing relative to her dress was in complete readiness, she considered that in another hour since there was so little a way to go, she might be there – . They were gone in Mr Stanley's carriage and therefore she might follow in her aunt's. As the plan seemed so very easy to be executed, and promising so much pleasure, it was after a few minutes deliberation finally adopted, and running up stairs, she rang in great haste for her maid. The bustle and hurry which then ensued for nearly an hour was at last happily concluded by her finding herself very well-dressed and in high beauty. Anne was then dispatched in the same haste to order the carriage, while her mistress was putting on her gloves, and arranging the folds of her dress. In a few minutes she heard the carriage drive up to the door, and tho' at first surprised at the expedition with which it had been got ready, she concluded after a little reflection that the men had received some hint of her intentions beforehand, and was hastening out of the room, when Anne came running into it in the greatest hurry and agitation, exclaiming 'Lord, ma'am! Here's a gentleman in a chaise and four come, and I cannot for the life conceive who it is! I happened to be crossing the hall when the carriage drove up, and I knew nobody would be in the way to let him in but Tom, and he looks so awkward you know, ma'am, now his hair is just done up, that I was not willing the gentleman should see him, and so I went to the door myself. And he is one of the handsomest young men you would wish to see; I was almost ashamed of being seen in my apron, ma'am, but however he is vastly handsome and did not seem to mind it at all. – And he asked me whether the family were at home; and so I said everybody was gone out but you, ma'am, for I would not deny you because I was sure you would like to see him. And then he asked me whether Mr and Mrs Stanley were not here, and so I said yes, and then – '

'Good Heavens!' said Kitty, 'what can all this mean! And who can it possibly be! Did you never see him before? And did not he tell you his name?'

'No, ma'am, he never said anything about it – So then I asked him to walk into the parlour, and he was prodigious agreeable, and – '

'Whoever he is,' said her mistress, 'he has made a great impression upon you, Nanny – But where did he come from? and what does he want here?'

'Oh! Ma'am, I was going to tell you, that I fancy his business is with you; for he asked me whether you were at leisure to see anybody, and desired I would give his compliments to you, and say he should be very happy to wait on you – However I thought he had better not come up into your dressing room, especially as everything is in such a litter, so I told him if he would be so obliging as to stay in the parlour, I would run up stairs and tell you he was come, and I dared to say that you would wait upon *him*. Lord, ma'am, I'd lay anything that he is come to ask you to dance with him tonight, and has got his chaise ready to take you to Mr Dudley's.'

Kitty could not help laughing at this idea, and only wished it might be true, as it was very likely that she would be too late for any other partner – 'But what, in the name of wonder, can he have to say to me? Perhaps he is come to rob the house – he comes in style at least; and it will be some consolation for our losses to be robbed by a gentleman in a chaise and four – . What livery has his servants?'

'Why that is the most wonderful thing about him, ma'am, for he has not a single servant with him, and came with hack horses; but he is as handsome as a Prince for all that, and has quite the look of one. Do, dear ma'am, go down, for I am sure you will be delighted with him – '

'Well, I believe I must go; but it is very odd! What can he have to say to me.' Then giving one look at herself in the glass, she walked with great impatience, tho' trembling all the while from not knowing what to expect, down stairs, and after pausing a moment at the door to gather courage for opening it, she resolutely entered the room. The stranger, whose appearance did not disgrace the account she had received of it from her maid, rose up on her entrance, and laying aside the newspaper he had been reading, advanced towards her with an air of the most perfect ease and vivacity, and said to her, 'It is certainly a very awkward circumstance to be thus obliged to introduce myself, but I trust that the necessity of the case will plead my excuse, and prevent your being prejudiced by it against me – . *Your* name, I need not ask, ma'am – . Miss Percival is too well known to me by description to need any information of that.' Kitty, who had been expecting him to tell his own name, instead of hers, and who from having been little in company, and never before in such a situation, felt herself unable to ask it, tho' she had been planning her speech all the way down stairs, was so confused and distressed by this unexpected address that she could only return a slight curtsy to it, and accepted the chair he reached her, without knowing what she did. The gentleman then continued. 'You are, I dare say, surprised to see me returned from France so soon, and nothing indeed but business could have brought me to England; a very melancholy affair has now occasioned it, and I was unwilling to leave it without payng my respects to the family in Devonshire whom I have so long wished to be acquainted with – .' Kitty, who felt much more surprised at his supposing her *to be so*, than at seeing a person in England, whose having ever left it was perfectly unknown to her, still continued silent from wonder and perplexity, and her visitor still continued to talk. 'You will suppose, madam, that I was not the *less* desirous of waiting on you, from your having Mr and Mrs Stanley with you – . I hope they are well? And Mrs Percival, how does *she* do?' Then without waiting for an answer he gaily added, 'But my dear Miss Percival, you are going out I am sure; and I am detaining you from your appointment. How can I ever expect to be forgiven for such injustice! Yet how can I, so circumstanced, forbear to offend! You seem dressed for a ball? But this is the land of gaiety I know; I have for many years been desirous of visiting it. You have dances I suppose at least every week – But where are the rest of your party gone, and what kind angel in compassion to me, has excluded *you* from it?'

'Perhaps sir,' said Kitty extremely confused by his manner of speaking to her, and highly displeased with the freedom of his conversation towards one who had never seen him before and did not *now* know his name, 'perhaps sir, you are acquainted with Mr and Mrs Stanley; and your business may be with *them*?'

'You do me too much honour, ma'am,' replied he laughing, 'in supposing me to be acquainted with Mr and Mrs Stanley; I merely know them by sight; very distant relations; only my father and mother. Nothing more I assure you.'

'Gracious Heaven!' said Kitty, 'are *you* Mr Stanley then?

– I beg a thousand pardons – Though really upon recollection I do not know for what – for you never told me your name – '

'I beg your pardon – I made a very fine speech when you entered the room, all about introducing myself; I assure you it was very great for *me*.'

'The speech had certainly great merit,' said Kitty smiling; 'I thought so at the time; but since you never mentioned your name in it, as an *introductory one* it might have been better.'

There was such an air of good humour and gaiety in Stanley, that Kitty, tho' perhaps not authorized to address him with so much familiarity on so short an acquaintance, could not forbear indulging the natural unreserve and vivacity of her own disposition, in speaking to him, as he spoke to her. She was intimately acquainted too with his family who were her relations, and she chose to consider herself entitled by the connexion to forget how little a while they had known each other. 'Mr and Mrs Stanley and your sister are extremely well,' said she, 'and will I dare say be very much surprised to see you – But I am sorry to hear that your return to England has been occasioned by an unpleasant circumstance.'

'Oh, don't talk of it,' said he, 'it is a most confounded shocking affair, and makes me miserable to think of it; But where are my father and mother, and your aunt gone? Oh! Do you know that I met the prettiest little waiting maid in the world, when I came here; she let me into the house; I took her for you at first.'

'You did me a great deal of honour, and give me more credit for good nature than I deserve, for I *never* go to the door when any one comes.'

'Nay do not be angry; I mean no offence. But tell me, where are you going to so smart? Your carriage is just coming round.'

'I am going to a dance at a neighbour's, where your family and my aunt are already gone.'

'Gone, without you! what's the meaning of *that*? But I suppose you are like myself, rather long in dressing.'

'I must have been so indeed, if that were the case for they have been gone nearly these two hours; The reason however was not what you suppose – I was prevented going by a pain – '

'By a pain!' interrupted Stanley, 'Oh! heavens, that is dreadful indeed! No matter where the pain was. But my dear Miss Percival, what do you say to my accompanying you? And suppose you were to dance with me too? *I* think it would be very pleasant.'

'I can have no objection to either I am sure,' said Kitty laughing to find how near the truth her maid's conjecture had been; 'on the contrary I shall be highly honoured by both, and I can answer for your being extremely welcome to the family who give the ball.'

'Oh! hang them; who cares for that; they cannot turn me out of the house. But I am afraid I shall cut a sad figure among all your Devonshire beaux in this dusty, travelling apparel, and I have not wherewithal to change it. You can procure me some powder perhaps, and I must get a pair of shoes from one of the men, for I was in such a devil of a hurry to leave Lyons that I had not time to have anything pack'd up but some linen.' Kitty very readily undertook to procure for him everything he wanted, and telling the footman to show him into Mr Stanley's dressing room, gave Nanny orders to send in some powder and pomatum, which orders Nanny chose to execute in person. As Stanley's preparations in dressing were confined to such very trifling articles, Kitty of course expected him in about ten minutes; but she found that it had not been merely a boast of vanity in saying that he was dilatory in that respect, as he kept her waiting for him above half an hour, so that the clock had struck ten before he entered the room and the rest of the party had gone by eight.

'Well,' said he as he came in, 'have not I been very quick? I never hurried so much in my life before.'

'In that case you certainly have,' replied Kitty, 'for all merit you know is comparative.'

'Oh! I knew you would be delighted with me for making so much haste – . But come, the carriage is ready; so, do not keep me waiting.' And so saying he took her by the hand, and led her out of the room.

'Why, my dear Cousin,' said he when they were seated, 'this will be a most agreeable surprise to everybody to see you enter the room with such a smart young fellow as I am – I hope your aunt won't be alarmed.'

'To tell you the truth,' replied Kitty, 'I think the best way to prevent it, will be to send for her, or your mother before we go into the room, especially as you are a perfect stranger, and must of course be introduced to Mr and Mrs Dudley – '

'Oh! Nonsense,' said he; 'I did not expect *you* to stand upon such ceremony; Our acquaintance with each other renders all such prudery, ridiculous; Besides, if we go in together, we shall be the whole talk of the country – '

'To *me*' replied Kitty, 'that would certainly be a most powerful inducement; but I scarcely know whether my aunt would consider it as such – . Women at her time of life, have odd ideas of propriety you know.'

'Which is the very thing that you ought to break them of; and why should you object to entering a room with me where all our relations are, when you have done me the honour to admit me without any chaperone into your carriage? Do not you think your aunt will be as much offended with you for one, as for the other of these mighty crimes?'

'Why really' said Catharine, 'I do not know but that she may; however, it is no reason that I should offend against decorum a second time, because I have already done it once.'

'On the contrary, that is the very reason which makes it impossible for you to prevent it, since you cannot offend for the *first time* again.'

'You are very ridiculous,' said she laughing, 'but I am afraid your arguments divert me too much to convince me.'

'At least they will convince you that I am very agreeable, which after all, is the happiest conviction for me, and as to the affair of propriety we will let that rest till we arrive at our journey's end – . This is a monthly ball I suppose. Nothing but dancing here – .'

'I thought I had told you that it was given by a Mr and Mrs Dudley – '

'Oh! aye so you did; but why should not Mr Dudley give one every month? By the bye who *is that* man? Everybody gives balls now I think; I believe I must give one myself soon – . Well, but how do you like my father and mother? And poor little Camilla too, has not she plagued you to death with the Halifaxes?' Here the carriage fortunately stopped at Mr Dudley's, and Stanley was too much engaged in handing her out of it, to wait for an answer, or to remember that what he had said required one. They entered the small vestibule which Mr Dudley had raised to the dignity of a hall, and Kitty immediately desired the footman who was leading the way upstairs, to inform either Mrs Percival, or Mrs Stanley of her arrival, and beg them to come to her, but Stanley unused to any contradiction and impatient to be amongst them, would neither allow her to wait, or listen to what she said, and forcibly seizing her arm within his, overpowered her voice with the rapidity of his own, and Kitty half angry, and half laughing was obliged to go with him up stairs, and could even with difficulty prevail on him to relinquish her hand before they entered the room.

Mrs Percival was at that very moment engaged in

conversation with a lady at the upper end of the room, to whom she had been giving a long account of her niece's unlucky disappointment, and the dreadful pain that she had with so much fortitude, endured the whole day – 'I left her however,' said she, 'thank heaven!, a little better, and I hope she has been able to amuse herself with a book, poor thing! for she must otherwise be very dull. She is probably in bed by this time, which while she is so poorly, is the best place for her you know, ma'am.' The lady was going to give her assent to this opinion, when the noise of voices on the stairs, and the footman's opening the door as if for the entrance of company, attracted the attention of every body in the room; and as it was in one of those intervals between the dances when every one seemed glad to sit down, Mrs Percival had a most unfortunate opportunity of seeing her niece whom she had supposed in bed, or amusing herself as the height of gaiety with a book, enter the room most elegantly dressed, with a smile on her countenance, and a glow of mingled cheerfulness and confusion on her cheeks, attended by a young man uncommonly handsome, and who without any of her confusion, appeared to have all her vivacity. Mrs Percival, colouring with anger and astonishment, rose from her seat, and Kitty walked eagerly towards her, impatient to account for what she saw appeared wonderful to every body, and extremely offensive to *her*, while Camilla on seeing her brother ran instantly towards him, and very soon explained who he was by her words and actions. Mr Stanley, who so fondly doted on his son, that the pleasure of seeing him again after an absence of three months prevented his feeling for the time any anger against him for returning to England without his knowledge, received him with equal surprise and delight; and soon comprehending the cause of his journey, forbore any further conversation with him, as he was eager to see his mother, and it was necessary that he should be introduced to Mr Dudley's family. This introduction to any one but Stanley would have been highly unpleasant, for they considered their dignity injured by his coming uninvited to their house, and received him with more than their usual haughtiness: But Stanley who with a vivacity of temper seldom subdued, and a contempt of censure not to be overcome, possessed an opinion of his own consequence, and a perseverance in his own schemes which were not to be damped by the conduct of others, appeared not to perceive it. The civilities therefore which they coldly offered, he received with a gaiety and ease peculiar to himself, and then attended by his father and sister walked into another room where his mother was playing at cards, to experience another meeting, and undergo a repetition of pleasure, surprise and explanations. While these were passing, Camilla eager to communicate all she felt to some one who would attend to her, returned to Catharine, and seating herself by her, immediately began – 'Well, did you ever know anything so delightful as this? But it always is so; I never go to a ball in my life but what something or other happens unexpectedly that is quite charming!'

'A ball' replied Kitty, 'seems to be a most eventful thing to you – '

'Oh! Lord, it is indeed – But only think of my brother's returning so suddenly – And how shocking a thing it is that has brought him over! I never heard anything so dreadful – !'

'What is it pray that has occasioned his leaving France? I am sorry to find that it is a melancholy event.'

'Oh! it is beyond anything you can conceive! His favourite hunter who was turned out in the park on his going abroad, somehow or other fell ill – No, I believe it was an accident, but however it was something or other, or else it was something else, and so they sent an express immediately to Lyons where my brother was, for they knew that he valued this mare more than anything else in the world besides; an so my brother set off directly for England, and without packing up another coat; I am quite angry with him about it; it was so shocking you know to come away without a change of clothes – '

'Why indeed,' said Kitty, 'it seems to have been a very shocking affair from beginning to end.'

'Oh! it is beyond anything you can conceive! I would rather have had *anything* happen than that he should have lost that mare.'

'Except his coming away without another coat.'

'Oh! yes, that has vexed me more than you can imagine. – Well, and so Edward got to Brampton just as the poor thing was dead; but as he could not bear to remain there *then*, he came off directly to Chetwynde on purpose to see us – . I hope he may not go abroad again.'

'Do you think he will not?'

'Oh! dear, to be sure he must, but I wish he may not with all my heart – . You cannot think how fond I am of him! By the bye are not you in love with him yourself?'

'To be sure I am,' replied Kitty laughing, 'I am in love with every handsome man I see.'

'That is just like me – *I* am always in love with every handsome man in the world.'

'There you outdo me,' replied Catharine 'for I am only in love with those I *do* see.' Mrs Percival who was sitting on the other side of her, and who began now to distinguish the words, *Love* and *handsome man*, turned hastily towards them and said 'What are you talking of, Catharine?' To which Catharine immediately answered with the simple artifice of a child, 'Nothing, ma'am.' She had already received a very severe lecture from her aunt on the imprudence of her behaviour during the whole evening; She blamed her for coming to the ball, for coming in the same carriage with Edward Stanley, and still more for entering the room with him. For the last-mentioned offence Catharine knew not what apology to give, and tho' she longed in answer to the second to say that she had not thought it would be civil to make Mr Stanley *walk*, she dared not so to trifle with her aunt, who would have been but the more offended by it. The first accusation however she considered as very unreasonable, as she thought herself perfectly justified in coming. This conversation continued till Edward Stanley entering the room came instantly towards her, and telling her that every one waited for *her* to begin the next dance led her to the top of the room, for Kitty, impatient to escape from so unpleasant a companion, without the least hesitation, or one civil scruple at being so distinguished, immediately gave him her hand, and joyfully left her seat. This conduct however was highly resented by several young ladies present, and among the rest by Miss Stanley whose regard for her brother tho' *excessive*, and whose affection for Kitty tho' *prodigious*, were not proof against such an injury to her importance and her peace. Edward had however only consulted his own inclinations in desiring Miss Percival to begin the dance, nor had he any reason to know that it was either wished or expected by anyone else in the party. As an heiress she was certainly of consequence, but her birth gave her no other claim to it, for her father had been a merchant. It was this very circumstance which rendered this unfortunate affair so offensive to Camilla, for tho' she would sometimes boast in the pride of her heart, and her eagerness to be admired that she did not know who her grandfather had been, and was as ignorant of everything relative to genealogy as to astronomy, (and she might have added, geography) yet she was really proud of her family and connexions, and easily offended if they were treated with neglect. 'I should not have minded it,' said she to her mother, 'if she had been *anybody* else's daughter; but to see her pretend to be above *me*, when her father was only a tradesman, is too bad! It is such an affront to our whole family! I declare I think Papa ought to interfere in it, but he never cares about anything but politics. If I were Mr Pitt or the Lord Chancellor, he would take care I should not be insulted, but he never thinks about *me*; And it is so provoking that *Edward* should let her stand there. I wish with all my heart that he had never come to England! I hope she may fall down and break her neck, or sprain her ankle.' Mrs Stanley perfectly agreed with her daughter concerning the affair, and tho' with less violence, expressed almost equal resentment at the indignity. Kitty in the meantime remained insensible of having given any one offence, and therefore unable either to offer an apology, or make a reparation; her whole attention was occupied by the happiness she enjoyed in dancing with the most elegant young man in the room, and every one else was equally unregarded. The evening indeed to *her*, passed off delightfully; he was her partner during the greatest part of it, and the united attractions that he possessed of person, address and vivacity, had easily gained that preference from Kitty which they seldom fail of obtaining from every one. She was too happy to care either for her aunt's ill humour which she could not help remarking, or for the alteration in Camilla's behaviour which forced itself at last on her observations. Her spirits were elevated above the influence of displeasure in any one, and she was equally indifferent as to the cause of Camilla's, or the continuance of her aunt's. Though Mr Stanley could never be really offended by any imprudence or folly in his son that had given him the pleasure of seeing him, he was yet perfectly convinced that Edward ought not to remain in England, and was resolved to hasten his leaving it as soon as possible; but when he talked to Edward about it, he found him much less disposed towards returning to France, than to accompany them in their projected tour, which he assured his father would be infinitely more pleasant to him, and that as to the affair of travelling he considered it of no importance, and what might be pursued at any little odd time, when he had nothing better to do. He advanced these objections in a manner which plainly showed that he had scarcely a doubt of their being complied with, and appeared to consider his father's arguments in opposition to them, as merely given with a view to keep up his authority, and such as he should find little difficulty in combating. He concluded at last by saying, as the chaise in which they returned together from Mr Dudley's reached Mrs Percival's, 'Well sir, we will settle this point some other time, and fortunately it is of so little consequence, that an immediate discussion of it is unnecessary.' He then got out of the chaise and entered the house without waiting for his father's reply.

It was not till their return that Kitty could account for that coldness in Camilla's behaviour to her, which had been so pointed as to render it impossible to be entirely unnoticed. When however they were seated in the coach with the two other ladies, Miss Stanley's indignation was no longer to be suppressed from breaking out into words, and found the following vent.

'Well, I must say *this*, that I never was at a stupider ball in my life! But it always is so; I am always disappointed in them for some reason or other. I wish there were no such things.'

'I am sorry, Miss Stanley,' said Mrs Percival drawing herself up, 'that you have not been amused; every thing was meant for the best I am sure, and it is a poor encouragement for your Mama to take you to another if you are so hard to be satisfied.'

'I do not know what you mean, ma'am, about Mama's *taking* me to another. You know I am come out.'

'Oh! dear Mrs Percival,' said Mrs Stanley, 'you must not believe everything that my lively Camilla says, for her spirits are prodigiously high sometimes, and she frequently speaks without thinking. I am sure it is impossible for *any one* to have been at a more elegant or agreeable dance, and so she wishes to express herself I am certain.'

'To be sure I do,' said Camilla very sulkily, 'only I must say that it is not very pleasant to have any body behave so rude to one as to be quite shocking! I am sure I am not at all offended, and should not care if all the world were to stand above me, but still it is extremely abominable, and what I cannot put up with. It is not that I mind it in the least, for I had just as soon stand at the bottom as at the top all night long, if it was not so very disagreeable – . But to have a person come in the middle of the evening and take everybody's place is what I am not used to, and tho' I do not care a pin about it myself, I assure you I shall not easily forgive or forget it.'

This speech which perfectly explained the whole affair to Kitty, was shortly followed on her side by a very submissive apology, for she had too much good sense to be proud of her family, and too much good nature to live at variance with any one. The excuses she made, were delivered with so much real concern for the offence, and such unaffected sweetness, that it was almost impossible for Camilla to retain that anger which had occasioned them; She felt indeed most highly gratified to find that no insult had been intended and that Catharine was very far from forgetting the difference in their birth for which she could *now* only pity her, and her good humour being restored with the same ease in which it had been affected, she spoke with the highest delight of the evening, and declared that she had never before been at so pleasant a ball. The same endeavours that had procured the forgiveness of Miss Stanley ensured to her the cordiality of her mother, and nothing was wanting but Mrs Percival's good humour to render the happiness of the others complete; but she, offended with Camilla for her affected superiority, still more so with her brother for coming to Chetwynde, and dissatisfied with the whole evening, continued silent and gloomy and was a restraint on the vivacity of her companions. She eagerly seized the very first opportunity which the next morning offered to her of speaking to Mr Stanley on the subject of his son's return, and after having expressed her opinion of its being a very silly affair that he came at all, concluded with desiring him to inform Mr Edward Stanley that it was a rule with her never to admit a young man into her house as a visitor for any length of time.

'I do not speak, sir,' she continued, 'out of any disrespect to you, but I could not answer it to myself to allow of his stay; there is no knowing what might be the consequence of it, if he were to continue here, for girls nowadays will always give a handsome young man the preference before any other, tho' for why, I never could discover, for what after all is youth and beauty? It is but a poor substitute for real worth and merit; Believe me Cousin that, what ever people may say to the contrary, there is certainly nothing like virtue for making us what we ought to be, and as to a young man's being young and handsome and having an agreeable person, it is nothing at all to the purpose for he had much better be respectable. I always *did* think so, and I always *shall*, and therefore you will oblige me very much by desiring your son to leave Chetwynde, or I cannot be answerable for what may happen between him and my niece. You will be surprised to hear *me* say it,' she continued, lowering her voice, 'but truth will out, and I must own that Kitty is one of the most impudent girls that ever existed. I assure you sir, that I have seen her sit and laugh and whisper with a young man whom she has not seen above half a dozen times. Her behaviour indeed is scandalous, and therefore I beg you will send your son away immediately, or everything will be at sixes and sevens.'

Mr Stanley, who from one part of her speech had scarcely known to what length her insinuations of Kitty's impudence were meant to extend, now endeavoured to quiet her fears on the occasion, by assuring her, that on every account he meant to allow only of his son's continuing that day with them, and that she might depend on his being more earnest in the affair from a wish of obliging her. He added also that he knew Edward to be very desirous himself of returning to France, as he wisely considered all time lost that did not forward the plans in which he was at present engaged, tho' he was but too well convinced of the contrary himself. His assurance in some degree quieted Mrs Percival, and left her tolerably relieved of her cares and alarms, and better disposed to behave with civility towards his son during the short remainder of his stay at Chetwynde. Mr Stanley went immediately to Edward, to whom he repeated the conversation that had passed between Mrs Percival and himself, and strongly pointed out the necessity of his leaving Chetwynde the next day, since his world was already engaged for it. His son however appeared struck only by the ridiculous apprehensions of Mrs Percival; and highly delighted at having occasioned them himself, seemed engrossed alone in thinking how he might increase them, without attending to any other part of his father's conversation. Mr Stanley could get no determinate answer from him, and tho' he still hoped for the best, they parted almost in anger on his side.

His son though by no means disposed to marry, or any otherwise attached to Miss Percival than as a good natured lively girl who seemed pleased with him, took infinite pleasure in alarming the jealous fears of her aunt by his attentions to her, without considering what effect they might have on the lady herself. He would always sit by her when she was in the room, appear dissatisfied if she left it, and was the first to enquire whether she meant soon to return. He was delighted with her drawings, and enchanted with her performance on the harpsichord; Everything that she said, appeared to interest him; his conversation was addressed to her alone, and she seemed to be the sole object of his attention. That such efforts should succeed with one so tremblingly alive to every alarm of the kind as Mrs Percival, is by no means unnatural, and that they should have equal influence with her niece whose imagination was lively, and whose disposition romantic, who was already extremely pleased with him, and of course desirous that he might be so with her, is as litle to be wondered at. Every moment as it added to the conviction of his liking her, made him still more pleasing, and strengthened in her mind a wish of knowing him better. As for Mrs Percival, she was in tortures the whole day; Nothing that she had ever felt before on a similar occasion was to be compared to the sensations which then distracted her; her fears had never been so strongly, or indeed so reasonably excited. – Her dislike of Stanley, her anger at her niece, her impatience to have them separated conquered every idea of propriety and good breeding, and though he had never mentioned any intention of leaving them the next day, she could not help asking him after dinner, in her eagerness to have him gone, at what time he meant to set out.

'Oh! Ma'am,' replied he, 'if I am off by twelve at night, you may think yourself lucky; and if I am not, you can only blame yourself for having left so much as the *hour* of my departure to my own disposal.' Mrs Percival coloured very highly at this speech, and without addressing herself to any one in particular, immediately began a long harangue on the shocking behaviour of modern young men, and the wonderful alteration that had taken place in them, since her time, which she illustrated with many instructive anecdotes of the decorum and modesty which had marked the characters of those whom she had known, when she had been young. This however did not prevent his walking in the garden with her niece, without any other companion for nearly an hour in the course of the evening. They had left the room for that purpose with Camilla at a time when Mrs Percival had been out of it, nor was it for some time after her return to it, that she could discover where they were. Camilla had taken two or three turns with them in the walk which led to the arbour, but soon growing tired of listening to a conversation in which she was seldom invited to join, and from its turning occasionally on books, very little able to do it, she left them together in the arbour, to wander alone to some other part of the garden, to eat the fruit, and examine Mrs Percival's greenhouse. Her absence was so far from being regretted, that it was scarcely noticed by them, and they continued conversing together on almost every subject, for Stanley seldom dwelt long on any, and had something to say on all, till they were interrupted by her aunt.

Kitty was by this time perfectly convinced that both in natural abilities, and acquired information, Edward Stanley was infinitely superior to his sister. Her desire of knowing that he was so, had induced her to take every opportunity of turning the conversation on history and they were very soon engaged in an historical dispute, for which no one was more calculated than Stanley who was so far from being really of any party, that he had scarcely a fixed opinion on the subject. He could therefore always take either side, and always argue with temper. In his indifference on all such topics he was very unlike his companion, whose judgement being guided by her feelings which were eager and warm, was easily decided, and though it was not always infallible, she defended it with a spirit and enthusiasm which marked her own reliance on it. They had continued therefore for sometime conversing in this manner on the character of Richard the Third, which he was warmly defending when he suddenly seized hold of her hand, and exclaiming with great emotion, 'Upon my honour you are entirely mistaken,' pressed it passionately to his lips, and ran out of the arbour. Astonished at this behaviour, for which she was wholly unable to account, she continued for a few moments motionless on the seat where he had left her, and was then on the point of following him up the narrow walk through which he had passed, when on looking up the one that lay immediately before the arbour, she saw her aunt walking towards her with more than her usual quickness. This explained at once the reason for his leaving her, but his leaving her in such manner was rendered still more inexplicable by it. She felt a considerable degree of confusion at having been seen by her in such a place with Edward, and at having that part of his conduct, for which she could not herself account, witnessed by one to whom all gallantry was odious. She remained therefore confused, distressed and irresolute, and suffered her aunt to approach her, without leaving the arbour.

Mrs Percival's looks were by no means calculated to animate the spirits of her niece, who in silence awaited her accusation, and in silence meditated her defence. After a few moments suspense, for Mrs Percival was too much fatigued to speak immediately, she began with great anger and asperity, the following harangue. 'Well; *this* is beyond anything I could have supposed. *Profligate* as I *knew* you to be, I was not prepared for such a sight. This is beyond any thing you ever did *before*; beyond any thing I ever heard of in my life! Such impudence, I never witnessed before in such a girl! And this is the reward for all the cares I have taken in your education; for all my troubles and anxieties; and Heaven knows how many they have been! All I wished for, was to breed you up virtuously; I never wanted you to play upon the harpsicord, or draw better than any one else; but I had hoped to see you respectable and good; to see you able and willing to give an example of modesty and virtue to the young people here abouts. I bought you Blair's *Sermons*, and Coelebs' *In Search of a Wife*, I gave you the key to my own library, and borrowed a great many good books of my neighbours for you, all to this purpose. But I might have spared myself the trouble – Oh! Catharine, you are an abandoned creature, and I do not know what will become of you. I am glad however,' she continued softening into some degreee of mildness, 'to see that you have some shame for what you have done, and if you are really sorry for it, and your future life is a life of penitence and reformation perhaps you may be forgiven. But I plainly see that every thing is going to sixes and sevens and all order will soon be at an end throughout the Kingdom.' 'Not however, ma'am, the sooner, I hope, from any conduct of mine,' said Catharine in a tone of great humility, 'for upon my honour I have done nothing this evening that can contribute to overthrow the establishment of the kingdom.'

'You are mistaken, child,' replied she; 'the welfare of every nation depends upon the virtue of its individuals, and any one who offends in so gross a manner against decorum and propriety is certainly hastening its ruin. You have been giving a bad example to the world, and the world is but too well disposed to receive such.'

'Pardon me, madam,' said her niece; 'but I *can* have given an example only to *you*, for you alone have seen the offence, Upon my world however there is no danger to fear from what I have done; Mr Stanley's behaviour has given me as much surprise, as it has done to you, and I can only suppose that it was the effect of his high spirits, authorized in his opinion by our relationship. But do you consider, madam, that it is growing very late? Indeed you had better return to the house.' This speech as she well knew, would be unanswerable with her aunt, who instantly rose, and hurried away under so many apprehensions for her own health, as banished for the time all anxiety about her niece, who walked quietly by her side, revolving within her own mind the occurrence that had given her aunt so much alarm. 'I am astonished at my own imprudence,' said Mrs Percival; 'How could I be so forgetful as to sit down out of doors at such a time of night? I shall certainly have a return of my rheumatism after it – I begin to feel very chill already. I must have caught a dreadful cold by this time – I am sure of being lain-up all the winter after it – ' Then reckoning with her fingers, 'Let me see; This is July; the cold weather will soon be coming in – August – September – October – November – December – January – February – March – April – Very likely I may not be tolerable again before May. I must and will have that arbour pulled down – it will be the death of me; who knows *now*, but what I may never recover – Such things *have* happened – My particular friend Miss Sarah Hutchinson's death was occasioned by nothing more – She stayed out late one evening in April, and got wet through for it rained very hard, and never changed her clothes when she came home – It is unknown how many people have died in consequence of catching cold! I do not believe there is a disorder in the world except the smallpox which does not spring from it.' It was in vain that Kitty endeavoured to convince her that her fears on the occasion were groundless; that it was not yet late enough to catch cold, and that even if it were, she might hope to escape any other complaint, and to recover in less than ten months. Mrs Percival only replied that she hoped she knew more of ill health than to be convinced in such a point by a girl who had always been perfectly well, and hurried up stairs leaving Kitty to make her apologies to Mr and Mrs Stanley for going to bed – . Tho' Mrs Percival seemed perfectly satisfied with the goodness of the apology herself, yet Kitty felt somewhat embarrassed to find that the only one she could offer to their visitors was that her aunt had *perhaps* caught cold, for Mrs Percival charged her to make light of it, for fear of alarming them. Mr and Mrs Stanley however who well knew that their cousin was easily terrified on that score, received the account of it with very little surprise, and all proper concern.

Edward and his sister soon came in, and Kitty had no difficulty in gaining an explanation of his conduct from him, for he was too warm on the subject himself, and too eager to learn its success, to refrain from making immediate enquiries about it; and she could not help feeling both surprised and offended at the ease and indifference with which he owned that all his intentions had been to frighten her aunt by pretending an affection for *her*, a design so very incompatible with that partiality which she had at one time been almost convinced of his feeling for her. It is true that she had not yet seen enough of him to be actually in love with him, yet she felt greatly disappointed that so handsome, so elegant, so lively a young man should be so perfectly free from any such sentiment as to make it his principal sport. There was a novelty in his character which to *her* was extremely pleasing; his person was uncommonly fine, his spirits and vivacity suited to her own, and his manners at once so animated and insinuating, that she thought it must be impossible for him to be otherwise than amiable, and was ready to give him credit for being perfectly so. He knew the powers of them himself; to them he had often been indebted for his father's forgiveness of faults which had he been awkward and inelegant would have appeared very serious; to them, even more than to his person or his fortune, he owed the regard which almost every one was disposed to feel for him, and which young women in particular were inclined to entertain.

Their influence was acknowledged on the present occasion by Kitty, whose anger they entirely dispelled, and whose cheerfulness they had power not only to restore, but to raise – . The evening passed off as agreeably as the one that had preceeded it; they continued talking to each other, during the chief part of it, and such was the power of his address, and the brilliancy of his eyes, that when they parted for the night, tho' Catharine had but a few hours before totally given up the idea, yet she felt almost convinced again that he was really in love with her. She reflected on their past conversation, and tho' it had been on various and indifferent subjects, and she could not exactly recollect any speech on his side expressive of such a partiality, she was still however nearly certain of its being so; But fearful of being vain enough to suppose such a thing without sufficient reason, she resolved to suspend her final determination on it, till the next day, and more especially till their parting which she thought would infallibly explain his regard if any he had – . The more she had seen of him, the more inclined was she to like him, and the more desirous that he should like *her*. She was convinced of his being naturally very clever and very well disposed, and that his thoughtlessness and negligence, which tho' they appeared to *her* as very becoming in *him*, she was aware would by mnay people be considered as defects in his character, merely proceeded from a vivacity always pleasing in young men, and were far from testifying a weak or vacant understanding. Having settled this point within herself, and being perfectly convinced by her own arguments of its truth, she went to bed in high spirits, determined to study his character, and watch his behaviour still more the next day.

She got up with the same good resolutions and would probably have put them in execution, had not Anne informed her as soon as she entered the room that Mr Edward Stanley was already gone. At first she refused to credit the information, but when her maid assured her that he had ordered a carriage the evening before to be there at seven o'clock in the morning and that she herself had actually seen him depart in it a little after eight, she could no longer deny her belief to it. 'And this,' thought she to herself blushing with anger at her own folly, 'this is the affection for me of which I was so certain. Oh! what a silly thing is woman! How vain, how unreasonable! To suppose that a young man would be seriously attached in the course of four and twenty hours, to a girl who has nothing to recommend her but a good pair of eyes! And he is really gone! Gone perhaps without bestowing a thought on me! Oh! why was not I up by eight o'clock? But it is a proper punishment for my laziness and folly, and I am heartily glad of it. I deserve it all, and ten times more for such insufferable vanity. It will at least be of service to me in that respect; it will teach me in future *not* to think every body is in love with me. Yet I *should* like to have seen him before he went, for perhaps it may be many years before we meet again. By his manner of leaving us however, he seems to have been perfectly indifferent about it. How very odd, that he should go without giving us notice of it, or taking leave of any one! But it is just like a young man, governed by the whim of the moment, or actuated merely by the love of doing anything odd! Unaccountable beings indeed! And young women are equally ridiculous! I shall soon begin to think like my aunt that everything is going to sixes and sevens, and that the whole race of mankind are degenerating.' She was just dressed, and on the point of leaving her room to make her personal enquires after Mrs Percival, when Miss Stanley knocked at her door, and on her being admitted began in her usual strain a long harangue upon her father's being so shocking as to make Edward go at all, and upon Edward's being so horrid as to leave them at such an hour in the morning. 'You have no idea,' said she, 'how surprised I was, when he came into my room to bid me good bye – '

'Have you seen him then, this morning?' said Kitty.

'Oh yes! And I was so sleepy that I could not open my eyes. And so he said, "Camilla, goodbye to you for I am going away – . I have not time to take leave of any body else, and I dare not trust myself to see Kitty, for then you know I should never get away – " '

'Nonsense,' said Kitty; 'he did not say that, or he was in joke if he did.'

'Oh! no I assure you he was as much in earnest as he ever was in his life; he was too much out of spirits to joke *then*. And he desired me when we all met at breakfast to give his compliments to your aunt, and his love to you, for you was a nice girl he said and he only wished it were in his power to be more with you. You were just the girl to suit him, because you were so lively and good-natured, and he wished with all his heart that you might not be married before he came back, for there was nothing he liked better than being here. Oh! You have no idea what fine things he said about you, till at last I fell asleep and he went away. But he certainly is in love with you – I am sure he is – I have thought so a great while I assure you.'

'How can you be so ridiculous?' said Kitty smiling with pleasure; 'I do not believe him to be so easily affected. But he *did* desire his love to me then? And wished I might not be married before his return? And said I was a nice girl, did he?'

'Oh! dear, yes, and I assure you it is the greatest praise in his opinion, that he can bestow on any body; I can hardly ever persuade him to call *me* one, tho' I beg him sometimes for an hour together.'

'And do you really think that he was sorry to go?'

'Oh! you can have no idea how wretched it made him. He would not have gone this month, if my father had not insisted on it; Edward told me so himself yesterday. He said that he wished with all his heart he had never promised to go abroad, for that he repented it more and more every day; that it interfered with all his other schemes, and that since Papa had spoke to him about it, he was more unwilling to leave Chetwynde than ever.'

'Did he really say all this? And why would your father insist upon his going?' 'His leaving England interfered with all his other plans, and his conversation with Mr Stanley had made him still more averse to it.' 'What can this mean?' 'Why that he is excessively in love with you to be sure; what other plans can he have? And I suppose my father said that if he had not been going abroad, he should have wished him to marry you immediately. – But I must go and see your aunt's plants – There is one of them that I quite dote on – and two or three more besides – '.

'Can Camilla's explanation be true?' said Catharine to herself, when her friend had left the room. 'And after all my doubts and uncertainties, can Stanley really be averse to leaving England for *my sake* only? "His plans interrupted." And what indeed can his plans be, but towards marriage? Yet *so soon* to be in love with me! – But it is the effect perhaps only of the warmth of heart which to *me* is the highest recommendation in any one. A heart disposed to love – And such under the appearance of so much gaiety and inattention, is Stanley's! Oh! how much does it endear him to me! But he is gone – gone perhaps for years – obliged to tear himself from what he most loves, his happiness is sacrificed to the vanity of his father! In what anguish he must have left the house! Unable to see me, or to bid me adieu, while I, senseless wretch, was daring to sleep. This, then explained his leaving us at such a time of day – He could not trust himself to see me – . Charming young man! How much must you have suffered! I *knew* that it was impossible for one so elegant, and so well bred, to leave any family in such a manner, but for a motive like this unanswerable.' Satisfied, beyond the power of change, of this, she went in high spirits to her aunt's apartment, without giving a moment's recollection on the vanity of young women, or the unaccountable conduct of young men.

Kitty continued in this state of satisfaction during the remainder of the Stanleys' visit – who took their leave with many pressing invitations to visit them in London, when as Camilla said, she might have an opportunity of becoming acquainted with that sweet girl Augusta Halifax – Or rather (thought Kitty,) of seeing my dear Mary Wynne again – . Mrs Percival in answer to Mrs Stanley's invitation replied – That she looked upon London as the hot house of vice where virtue had long been banished from society and wickedness of every description was daily gaining ground – that Kitty was of herself sufficiently inclined to give way to, and indulge in vicious inclinations – and therefore was the last girl in the world to be trusted in London, as she would be totally unable to withstand temptation – .

After the departure of the Stanleys Kitty returned to her usual occupations, but alas! they had lost their power of pleasing. Her bower alone retained its interest in her feelings, and perhaps that was owing to the particular remembrance it brought to her mind of Edward Stanley.

The summer passed away unmarked by any incident worth narrating, or any pleasure to Catharine save one, which arose from the receipt of a letter from her friend Cecilia now Mrs Lascelles, announcing the speedy return of herself and husband to England.

A correspondence productive indeed of little pleasure to either party had been established between Camilla and Catharine. The latter had now lost the only satisfaction she had ever received from the letters of Miss Stanley, as that young lady having informed her friend of the departure of her brother to Lyons now never mentioned his name – her letters seldom contained any intelligence except a description of some new article of dress, an enumeration of various

 engagements, a panegyric on Augusta Halifax and perhaps

a little abuse of the unfortunate Sir Peter – .

The Grove, for so was the mansion of Mrs Percival at Chetwynde denominated, was situated within five miles from Exeter, but though that lady possessed a carriage and horses of her own, it was seldom that Catharine could prevail on her to visit that town for the purpose of shopping, on account of the many officers perpetually quartered there and who infested the principal streets – . A company of strolling players on their way from some neighbouring races having opened a temporary theatre there, Mrs Percival was prevailed on by her niece to indulge her by attending the performance once during their stay – Mrs Percival insisted on paying Miss Dudley the compliment of inviting her to join the party, when a new difficulty arose, from the necessity of having some gentleman to attend them – .

A Note on Jane Austen

Jane Austen was born at Steventon, Hampshire, in 1775, the daughter of a clergyman. At the age of nine she was sent to school at Reading with her elder sister Cassandra, who was her lifelong friend and confidante, but she was largely taught by her father. She began to write for recreation while still in her teens. In 1801 the family moved to Bath, the scene of so many episodes in her books and, after the death of her father in 1805, to Southampton and then to the village of Chawton, near Alton in Hampshire. Here she lived uneventfully until May 1817, when the family moved to Winchester seeking skilled medical attention for her ill-health, but she died two months later. She is buried in Winchester Cathedral.

Her best-known novels are *Sense and Sensibility* (1811), *Pride and Prejudice* (1813), *Mansfield Park* (1814), *Emma* (1816), and *Northanger Abbey* and *Persuasion*, both published posthumously in 1818.